Is That Josie?

Keiko Narahashi

Margaret K. McElderry Books
New York
Maxwell Macmillan Canada
Toronto
Maxwell Macmillan International
New York   Oxford   Singapore   Sydney

For Joy
with thanks to Micah

Margaret K. McElderry Books
Macmillan Publishing Company
866 Third Avenue
New York, NY 10022

Maxwell Macmillan Canada, Inc.
1200 Eglinton Avenue East
Suite 200
Don Mills, Ontario M3C 3N1

Macmillan Publishing Company is part of the Maxwell Communication Group of Companies.
First edition
Printed in Hong Kong by South China Printing Company (1988) Ltd.
The text of this book is set in Aldine 401.

10 9 8 7 6 5 4 3 2 1
The illustrations are rendered in watercolor.

Library of Congress Catalog Card Number: 93-81163

ISBN 0-689-50606-6

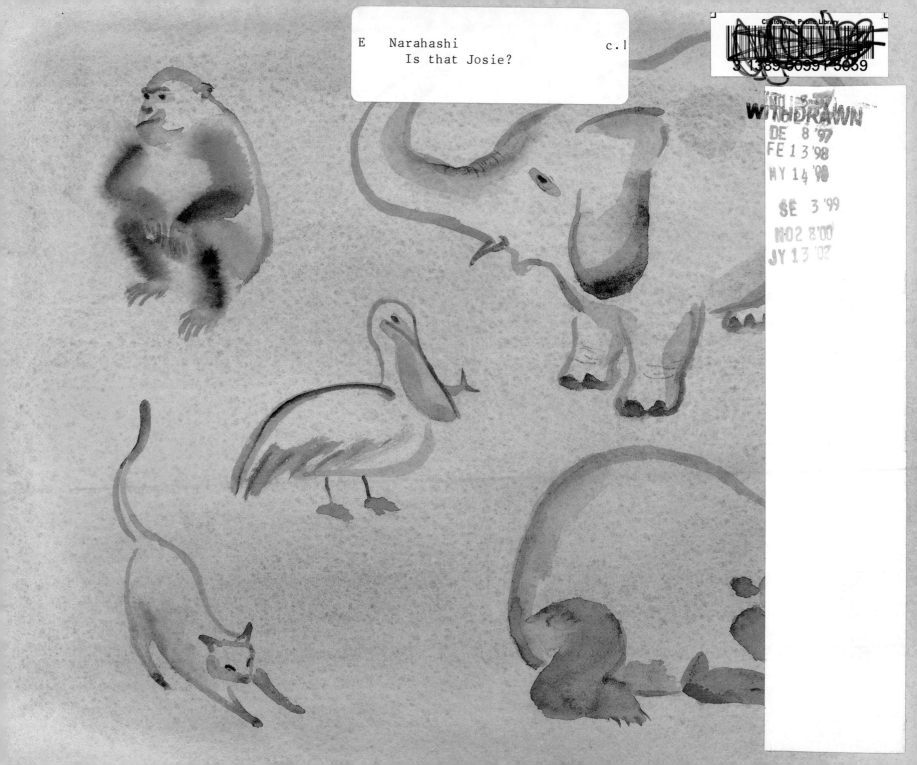

Written and illustrated by Keiko Narahashi
I Have a Friend

Illustrated by Keiko Narahashi

Who Said Red? by Mary Serfozo
Who Wants One? by Mary Serfozo
Rain Talk by Mary Serfozo
The Little Band by James Sage
My Grandfather's Hat by Melanie Scheller
The Magic Purse by Yoshiko Uchida

Is that Josie peeking out of bed?

No, it's a sly fox hiding in her den.

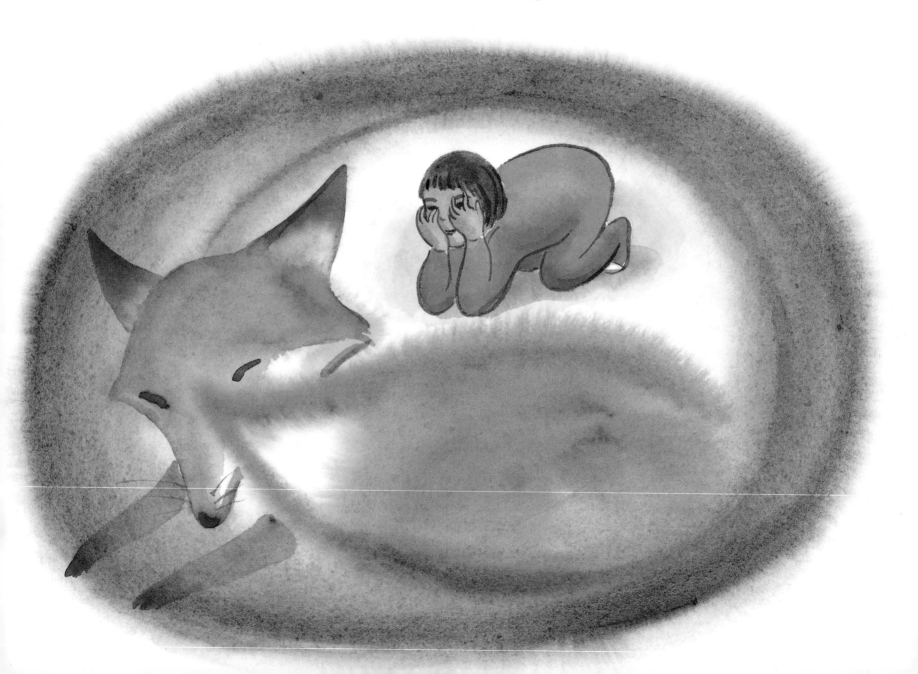

Is that Josie in those green and yellow stripes?

No, it's a turtle. Peekaboo, where are you?

Is that Josie thumping down the stairs?

No, it's a kangaroo with her baby in her pouch.

Is that Josie with her blocks stacked high?

No, it's a tiny busy ant in a busy anthill.

Is that Josie dangling down her daddy's back?

No, it's a little possum. Hang on tight, here we go!

Is that Josie running fast through the grass?

No, it's a cheetah. There she goes—wait for us!

Is that Josie way up high on a swing?

No, it's an eagle soaring high and swooping low.

Is that Josie eating blueberry pie?

No, it's a hippopotamus. Bye-bye, pie!

Is that Josie making waves in her bath?

No, it's a dolphin diving deep.

Is that Josie brushing her shiny white teeth?

Oh, no, it's a crocodile with a GREAT, BIG, W-I-D-E smile!

And is *this* Josie all ready for bed?

YES! It's Mommy's big girl. Hug her tight.

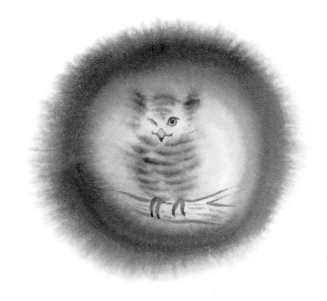

Good night.